Born to be Wild
Little Dolphins

Valérie Guidoux

Words that appear in the glossary are printed in
boldface type the first time they occur in the text.

GARETH**STEVENS**
PUBLISHING
A Member of the WRC Media Family of Companies

Born underwater

A baby dolphin is born in the open ocean and does not have any shelter, but it stays well protected, cuddled next to its mother's soft skin. When the little dolphin, or calf, is hungry, it pushes its beak against its mother's body to get a drink of warm milk, which flows from underneath her stomach. As the calf drinks, it swims along and often rises to the surface of the water with its mother.

A mother dolphin gives birth to one calf at a time. Another female helps her protect and raise the newborn calf, acting like the little dolphin's aunt.

What do you think?

Why do dolphins often swim up to the surface of the water?

a) because they love to play in the waves

b) because they like to watch the boats

c) because they need to take a breath of air

Dolphins swim up to the surface of the water to take a breath of air.

Like humans, dolphins are **mammals**. They feed their babies milk and cannot breathe underwater. A dolphin never dives for very long, usually not for more than a few minutes. It breathes through a small hole, called a **blowhole**, on the top of its head. When the dolphin's head is above the water, the blowhole opens and closes to take in air. A dolphin holds its breath to swim underwater. When dolphins come up to breathe, they will often jump and play in the waves, too.

As soon as a dolphin calf is born, its mother and another female push it to the surface of the water so it can take its first breath.

When a dolphin breaks the surface of the water, it opens its blowhole to breathe out, then breathes in deeply before diving underwater again.

4

Dolphins breathe only one to four times a minute. When a dolphin is underwater, its blowhole is always closed. Some kinds of dolphins can hold their breath and stay underwater for up to fifteen minutes!

Racing through the Ocean

Even though a little dolphin is not a fish, it is still a swimming champion. With a body shaped like a rocket, it can cut through water, which slides easily over the dolphin's soft, smooth skin. At the end of its body is a tail called a caudal **fin**. A dolphin uses its large, fan-shaped tail to move forward and to stop. By following its mother, a young dolphin quickly learns how to jump and spin in the waves. When the dolphin becomes an adult, it will be able to swim up to 30 miles (48 kilometers) an hour.

What do you think?

When dolphins are swimming very fast, how do they keep from bumping into fish?

a) They see the fish coming and change the direction they are swimming in.

b) They have a kind of **sonar** system that tells them where the fish are.

c) They know how to stop and move out of the way quickly.

A dolphin spends its time diving below the surface of the water and leaping above it. The dolphin moves its horizontal tail up and down to **propel** itself through the water.

Dolphins have a kind of sonar system that tells them where the fish are.

When their heads are above water, dolphins use sight to know what is nearby. But the deeper dolphins swim, the darker the water is, and the harder it is for them to see. While a dolphin swims, it constantly makes clicking sounds. The clicks travel very quickly through the water as **sound waves**, which bounce off of rocks, fish, and other animals or objects. Like **echoes**, the sounds travel back to the dolphin, helping it figure out what is in front of it.

Because its eyes are on the sides of its head, a dolphin cannot see things in front of it very well. To see an object well, it often moves sideways.

Under a dolphin's rounded forehead is a body part called the "melon," which helps produce the clicking sounds a dolphin makes and picks up the echoes that bounce back.

Dolphins have excellent hearing. They can hear noises from waves, boats, and almost any creature in the water. Dolphins have small ear openings hidden behind their eyes, but most of the sounds they hear travel to their middle and inner ears through their jaws.

A dolphin's tail muscles are very strong and powerful. The dolphin uses the two flippers on its chest for steering and the **dorsal fin** on its back for balance.

Fishing with Friends

A dolphin calf drinks its mother's milk for about eighteen months. At six months of age, however, it also starts to eat a few fish. When the calf is older, it will learn to hunt with the other dolphins. Sometimes, dozens of dolphins will hunt as a group, chasing after **sardines**. A little dolphin and its mother swim a short distance away from the group, watching and enjoying the hunting show.

Like all mammals, dolphins are warm-blooded animals. They must eat often because they need a lot of energy to swim and to keep their body temperatures the same in both cool and warm water.

What do you think?

How do dolphins eat sardines?

a) They swallow them whole.

b) They sort out the biggest, then eat them one by one.

c) They carefully chew them until they are mashed up.

Dolphins eat sardines by swallowing them whole.

Dolphins hunt for food together. As soon as they spot a school, or large group, of fish, all the dolphins begin to act. Each dolphin in the group has a job. They herd the fish up to the surface of the water, surrounding them on all sides so none of the fish can escape. Soon, the waves are rippling with thousands of confused fish, and the dolphins start swallowing the feast.

Both dolphins and tuna eat small fish. Groups of dolphins will often swim alongside tuna when they hunt.

A dolphin has about one hundred pointed teeth, which it uses to grab fish before swallowing them. Dolphins do not need to chew their food because their stomachs have a pouch that grinds up the food.

12

Always in a Good Mood

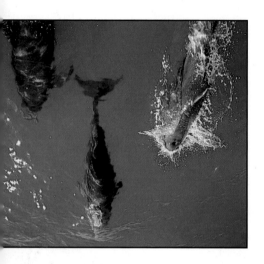

Little dolphins are always chattering to their friends with whistles, squeaks, creaks, and clicks. Splash! Splash! One dolphin jumps out of the water and crashes down again, calling to the others. There is a boat on the water, and the dolphin wants its friends to come race with it. Humans love to see dolphins swimming next to their boats, and dolphins seem to like humans, too.

What do you think?

Why do dolphins like to swim in front of boats?

a) because they are attracted to the sailors' songs

b) because they want to swim in the waves made by the boats

c) because they think the sailors might throw them some food

When dolphins see a boat, they will often swim alongside and in front of it, leaping and jumping in the waves.

Dolphins want to swim in the waves made by boats.

Slicing through the water with its **bow**, a boat creates waves, and dolphins love to swim in them. Dolphins often use the stream of waves to race with the boat. When they are not racing boats or hunting for food, both young dolphins and adult dolphins spend a lot of time playing or cuddling together, while talking to each other in their own language. Sometimes, male dolphins will argue or fight with each other, making loud clicks with their beaks.

Dolphins seem to love to swim fast. When they come to the surface to breathe, they often jump over waves to go even faster.

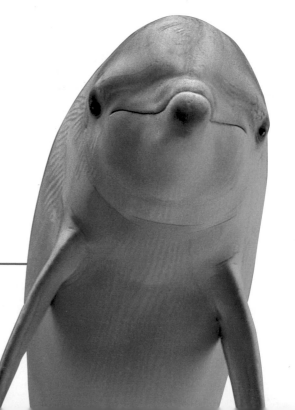

The shape of a dolphin's mouth makes the dolphin looks as if it is smiling. A dolphin is a friendly animal, but it does not really smile.

Dolphins have soft, sensitive skin and a very strong sense of touch. While they swim, they constantly rub their bodies together and stroke each other with their flippers and tails.

Staying Close Together

By the time a little dolphin grows up, it has learned not to be afraid of storms, humans, boats, or the giant whales that swim near it in the ocean. Its mother has taught it, however, not to trust white sharks and to stay away from the pointed fins of killer whales. The dolphin has also learned that, for the best protection in the wide, deep ocean, it should always stay close to its family or friends.

Groups of dolphins protect mothers and their calves. A group will take care of its sick animals and will never leave an injured dolphin behind.

What do you think?

What do father dolphins do to help raise their young?

a) They teach the young calves how to hunt.

b) They never take care of their young.

c) They live alone, away from their families.

Father dolphins never take care of their young.

Usually, several females and their young live together, but the males come and go. Both males and females **mate** with more than one partner so they do not know which dolphin is the father of each calf. Male dolphins sometimes live by themselves, but they still hunt with a group.

A female dolphin gives birth to one calf every two to three years. A calf usually stays with its mother for three to six years, even after she has given birth again.

Female dolphins are ready to mate when they are nine or ten years old. Males, however, do not mate until they are ten or twelve years old.

Dolphins live in groups of two to twenty dolphins, but these small groups sometimes gather together, forming a group of more than one hundred animals.   In large groups, dolphins can hunt more successfully and better protect themselves against danger.

Dolphins are marine mammals, which means they live in water. They live close to the shore, in areas of warm or **tropical** seas. Dolphins in the wild usually live about thirty years, although some can live as long as fifty years. An adult dolphin weighs between 300 and 1,300 pounds (135 and 600 kilograms).

There are about forty kinds of dolphins in the world. Dolphins are related to porpoises and whales.

The openings of a dolphin's ears are small holes hidden behind its eyes.

From their beaks to their tails, dolphins are between 6 and 13 feet (2 and 4 meters) long.

A dolphin's tail, or caudal fin, is horizontal. The dolphin pumps its tail up and down to move forward.

A dolphin breathes through its blowhole, which is a small hole on the top of its head.

With its eyes on the sides of its head, a dolphin cannot see objects directly in front of it very well.

A dolphin's beak is about 6 inches (15 centimeters) long. The bottle-nosed dolphin, which is the most well-known kind of dolphin, is named for the shape of its **snout**.

A dolphin uses its flippers to steer. Along with its tail, flippers help the dolphin stop, too.

GLOSSARY

blowhole — the breathing hole on the tops of the heads of some marine mammals

bow — the front of a boat

dorsal fin — the fin on the backs of some water animals

echoes — repeated sounds, made when sound waves meet objects and bounce off of them

fin — one of the thin, flat parts that stick out of the bodies of marine animals such as dolphins

mammals — warm-blooded animals that have backbones, give birth to live babies, feed their young with milk from the mother's body, and have skin that is usually covered with hair or fur

mate — (v) to join together to produce young

propel — to move forward with a forceful motion

sardines — any of several kinds of small, oily fish

snout — the long part of an animal's face that sticks out from its head like a nose

sonar — a method of using echoes to determine the locations of objects underwater

sound waves — movements of sound that travel through air, water, or solid materials

tropical — of or related to the warmest regions of Earth

Please visit our web site at: **www.garethstevens.com**
For a free color catalog describing Gareth Stevens Publishing's list of high-quality books and multimedia programs, call 1-800-542-2595 (USA) or 1-800-387-3178 (Canada). Gareth Stevens Publishing's fax: (414) 332-3567.

Library of Congress Cataloging-in-Publication Data

Guidoux, Valérie.
  [Petit dauphin. English]
  Little dolphins / Valérie Guidoux. — North American ed.
    p. cm. — (Born to be wild)
  ISBN 0-8368-4735-0 (lib. bdg.)
  1. Bottlenose dolphin—Infancy—Juvenile literature. I. Title. II. Series.
QL737.C432G85 2005
599.53'139—dc22   2004065367

This North American edition first published in 2006 by
Gareth Stevens Publishing
A Member of the WRC Media Family of Companies
330 West Olive Street, Suite 100
Milwaukee, Wisconsin 53212 USA

First published in 2000 as *Le petit dauphin* by Mango Jeunesse, an imprint of Editions Mango, Paris, France.

Picture Credits (t = top, b = bottom, l = left, r = right)
Bios: Jeffrey L. Rotman 10. Jacana: cover; Tom Walker title page, 9(t); Yves Gladu 14; Westmorland 15; Norbert Wu 18. Mango: 20(both); PHONE: François Gohier 6, 7, 8(t) back cover; Jeff Jacobsen 12. Sunset: Gérard Lacz 2, 4(both), 5, 13, 16(b), 17, 22, 22–23; ANT 8(b), 9(b), Weststock 16(t), D. Perrine 21.

English translation: Muriel Castille
Gareth Stevens editor: Barbara Kiely Miller
Gareth Stevens art direction: Tammy West
Gareth Stevens designer: Jenni Gaylord

Printed in the United States of America

1 2 3 4 5 6 7 8 9 09 08 07 06 05